THE APPLE ARGUMENT

This book is for Joni Sussman and Elizabeth Harding,
both part of my firmament.
—J.Y.

To my best friend, Lisa, a great nature lover
—A.B.

KAR-BEN PUBLISHING®
An imprint of Lerner Publishing Group, Inc.
241 First Avenue North
Minneapolis, MN 55401 USA

Website address: www.karben.com

Main body text set in Bailey Sans.
Typeface provided by Internation Typeface Corp.

Library of Congress Cataloging-in-Publication Data

Names: Yolen, Jane, author. | Barghigiani, Anita, 1987- illustrator.
Title: The apple argument / Jane Yolen ; illustrated by Anita Barghigiani.
Description: Minneapolis, MN, U.S.A. : Kar-Ben Publishing, [2024] | Audience: Ages 3–7 | Audience: Grades
    K–1 | Summary: "In the Garden of Eden, God buried the vegetables and put the fruits where they could be
    seen. Wanting easy picking, the caretakers of the Garden listen to the snake, pick the apples, and suffer the
    consequences"— Provided by publisher.
Identifiers: LCCN 2023004762 (print) | LCCN 2023004763 (ebook) | ISBN 9781728486451 (library binding) |
    ISBN 9798765613351 (epub)
Subjects: LCSH: Eden—Juvenile literature. | Creation—Juvenile literature. | Adam (Biblical figure)—Juvenile
    literature. | Eve (Biblical figure)—Juvenile literature. | Bible stories, English—Genesis—Juvenile literature.
Classification: LCC BS1237 .Y65 2024 (print) | LCC BS1237 (ebook) | DDC 222/.11—dc23/eng/20230516

LC record available at https://lccn.loc.gov/2023004762
LC ebook record available at https://lccn.loc.gov/2023004763

Manufactured in China
1-52563-50755-4/10/2023

The
APPLE
ARGUMENT

Jane Yolen

illustrated by
Anita Barghigiani

KAR-BEN
PUBLISHING

It was dark,
years ago,
centuries,
ages,
eons.

Though time did not exist yet.

And then God made blinking lights:

sun,
moon,
planets,
stars,
so many of them,
but none with names.

Just "beautiful blinking lights."

And then on one particular
tiny blinking light,
God made a garden.
Though it wasn't yet called a garden,
since it was the very first one.
God called it Eden.

Then God buried things in the fertile ground:
red and white and brown and orange.
God called them Vegetables,
which is a funny name for
whatever-they-were.

And then God made even brighter things,
which grow on trees and vines.
Some of them smelled sweet.
Some of them smelled tart.
Some of them had no smell at all.
God called them Fruits
and gave each its own name.

And then something moved
in the heavens.
It fell to Eden
and then silently wiggled
and wriggled away,
quietly giggling,
into the undergrowth.

The Snake.
The Fruits did not see it.

The Fruits were having an argument.
Apple was the first to speak.

"I am hardiest," Apple said.
"I am best."

"I am biggest!" said Pomegranate.
"I am best."

"I am sweetest," said
Grape. "I am best."

"No—I am yummiest," said Fig. "I am best."

"I can make all of you taste even better with just one drop," said Citron.

No one won the argument.
No one lost the argument.
But each Fruit felt that it had won.
Especially Apple.

They kept arguing
Until God told them,

"ENOUGH!"

But it was not enough.
The argument continued.

So God said to the Fruits,
"I will make two caretakers
to listen to your arguments.
And I will move far away
so I do not need to hear you.
One caretaker will be a man
and one a woman."

God showed the caretakers
how to do their job,
which was to take care of the garden,
and how to dig out the Vegetables
for their meals.
God wanted to teach the caretakers to work hard.
God told them
to *never* eat the Fruits.
"Vegetables, yes. Fruits, no," God warned them.

But the caretakers did not want to work hard,
and digging out the Vegetables was hard.
It was easier to pluck the Fruits
from trees and vines.
Wanting things to be easy
became the first real problem in the garden.

The Fruits enticed the caretakers.
"Eat me! Eat me!" they all cried.
"I am hardiest," said Apple.
"I am biggest," said Pomegranate.
"I am sweetest," said Grape.
"I am yummiest," said Fig.
"I can make all of them taste even better
with just one drop," said Citron.

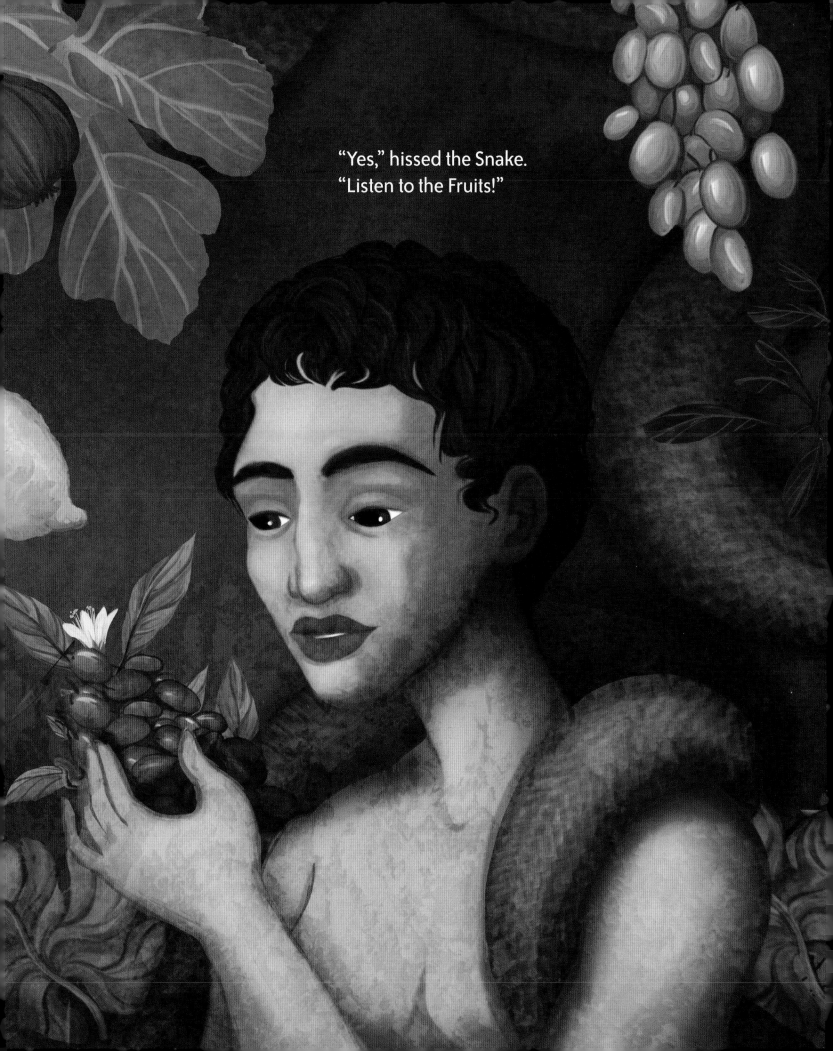

And because the caretakers were closer to the Fruits
than to God,
they could hear the Fruits speak.
But they did not know the Fruits' language.
So, because it was the easiest thing to do,
they tried all the different Fruits.
Apple *was* the hardiest,
Grape the sweetest,
Fig the yummiest.
Pomegranate was the most difficult to eat
because knives had not been invented yet,
only fingers.
And a squeeze of Citron made all of them taste even better.

But because the caretakers did not listen to God's warnings
or because they didn't like to do hard work
or because they listened to the Snake,
God took them all—caretakers, Fruits, and Vegetables—out of the garden
and put them on the blinking light God called Earth.

Where Fruits did not grow all year-round,
and gardening always had to begin
with hard work
of digging and planting.

And no one noticed the Snake
that went wriggling and giggling
into the undergrowth.
Well, God noticed, but God didn't tell anyone.

Those caretakers were our ancestors.
We taught ourselves how to work the land.
But—like the Fruits—we argue.
And like the Fruits, we are hardy, sweet, and difficult.
And like the Fruits, we have both good tastes and bad.

And some of us make all of us a little bit better.

Author's Note
This is modern midrash, a made-up story
based on the Garden of Eden story in Torah.
It might explain a lot of things.

About the Author
Jane Yolen lives in Massachusetts and has written more than four hundred
books across all genres and age ranges, including the Sydney Taylor Honor
book *Miriam at the River.* In 2022 she was named the Sydney Taylor Body-of-
Work Winner. She has been called the Hans Christian Andersen of America
and the Aesop of the twentieth century.

About the Illustrator
Anita Barghigiani was born near Pisa, Italy. She is a graduate of the Academy
of Fine Arts of Florence. When she attended the Bologna Children's Book Fair
for the first time, she fell in love with children's books and decided to study
illustration and entertainment design. She lives in Florence where she works,
plays the guitar, and volunteers helping animals.